Recruitment

AMY LAURENS

OTHER WORKS

Find other works by the author at www.amylaurens.com

Recruitment

INKLET #97

AMY LAURENS

Inkprint
PRESS
www.inkprintpress.com

Print ISBN: 978-1-922434-47-0
eBook ISBN: 9798201911867

www.inkprintpress.com

National Library of Australia Cataloguing-in-Publication Data
Laurens, Amy 1985 –
Recruitment
40 p.
ISBN: 978-1-922434-47-0
Inkprint Press, Canberra, Australia
1. Fiction—Fantasy—Contemporary 2. Fiction—Fantasy—Urban 3. Fiction—Fantasy—Dragons & Mythical Creatures 4. Fiction—Short Stories

First Print Edition: November 2022
Cover photo © rdrgraphe via Deposit Photos
Cover design © Inkprint Press
Interior art © Amy Laurens

RECRUITMENT

*T*HE FIRST THING YOU NOTICED ABOUT Dave was his eyes: bright, piercing blue beneath a shock of light brown hair, capable of drilling right into your soul. They weren't kind, per se, but you looked into them and knew that you were seen, as you were, the good, the bad—and the secret.

Luckily for Dave, this ability actually worked: not only could he make you feel seen, he did actually see you. Whether you wanted him to or not. Whether you were supposed to be visible or not.

He was recruited early on because of that.

A bead of sweat rolled down Dave's temple as he crouched beneath a black-trunked eucalypt, the shade barely cooler, the dusk barely dimmer. It was half past eight on a Friday evening, and the sun was only just farewelling the day with a blush of hot orange on the hot, summer horizon of bare rolling hills outside the city. The air carried the smells of the city far beyond its borders—hot oil, hot concrete, hot asphalt, hot fuel.

He glanced at his watch and noted absently that his fair skin was already considering burning, despite the late hour of the day.

Eight thirty-one. They were late.

Dave wasn't sure who, exactly, were late; he'd been handed a blank envelope by the woman with the serious soul and told that it was a test, that if he could do what they hoped he could, he'd be hired.

That was it. Literally all the information he'd been given.

The envelope contained only a date and a time, and a contract stipulating abject secrecy and an excellent pay rate, even for this test, with the promise of significant on-going employment benefits if he passed.

He had no idea how he was supposed to pass, because he had no idea what they expected him to do.

But Dave's fridge had been empty for going on a week now, and only sporadically full for a month before that. The conflict with the fey was finally sinking its long fingers into the common populace; no longer a novel news item, the fey had been hitting hard at supply lines, trying to disrupt agriculture, industry, transport... and civilians globally were beginning to suffer.

So it had barely been a choice. Un-informative the envelope might have been, but Dave knew a military stance when he saw one, and a military pay cheque was a secure one.

He wiped away the bead of sweat from his temple, inhaled deeply of the city-tainted air that also smelled a little of baked eucalypt and hot dirt—hot everything, everything was hot, his body was soaked in sweat and he could almost bring himself to long for his sporadically air-conditioned bedroom, if not for that tantalising promise of pay—and checked the time again.

Eight thirty-two.

Ahead, up the road toward the horizon, something shimmered. For a moment, he hoped it was simply a trick of the dying light, a mirage in the heat, the orange dirt of the road shining briefly.

But the shimmer persisted—and not only that, it began to creep closer.

Dave's heart leapt to his throat, and suddenly the test made sense. He didn't know anyone else who could see through a fey glamour; of course the military would want to recruit him.

But... Now what? What was he supposed to *do*, now that he'd spotted an in-coming glamour?

Unarmed. Uninformed.

Dave shook his head and exhaled sniffily.

Briefly, he cast about for a way to hide; he'd been sensible enough to wear camel-coloured pants and a grey-brown shirt, nondescript, the best he had for camouflage, but right now, it seemed pressing that he find something better. Unfortunately, he was surrounded by a flat expanse of dirt all the way to the sloping horizon, with only a few tall trees that offered little in the way of visible obstruction in the drought-dry plain. Even the grass was yellowed, turning crunchy at the tips, and short of digging himself down into the ground, there was nothing to be done.

He didn't chew his lip, because that would have shown uncertainty (and he had no idea if his prospective employers were observing him in some way), but he did let his hands tighten briefly into fists.

The shimmer drew closer still, maybe fifty or forty metres now, hard to say exactly without having walked the path himself, but that log there, the fallen, blackened one by the path up the slope… He squinted at the trunk of the tree next to him, rough, black bark darkening as dusk left the sky and twilight encroached.

Yes. He'd lay good money that the log was about the same thickness as the gum tree he stood beside, which made the shimmer about forty metres distant.

Can't run.

Can't hide.

He swallowed, mouth suddenly dry as the dust he could taste.

The eastern sky behind him had dimmed to navy, now, and the fading light wasn't making it easier to track the shimmer that approached, and with every passing second his heart pounded louder in his chest, adrenalin ramping up as if to fight or flee.

Thirty metres.

Twenty.

The glamour resolved, close enough now that he could not only spot it, but see through it: two of the fey themselves, one of whom Dave thought he possibly recognised from the anti-fey propaganda posters around town and on TV.

Important, then, if they had her on the posters. That was the olive-skinned one on the right, the tall female with the dark, curling hair and the long, strong nose.

The brown-skinned one on the left didn't seem familiar at all, though he wore the sleeveless leather vest that seemed traditional among fey males, with loose, billowy pants that seemed enviably cool in this abominable heat.

Dave could taste the salt of sweat on his lips, and right now he couldn't have said for sure whether the sweat was entirely due to the heat—or if, perhaps, some fear had crept in there as well.

Ten metres away, ten longish paces. Heart thumping, he twisted and stared up at the eucalypt, as though the black-trunked tree was the most interesting thing he'd ever seen (and, to be fair, the jagged silhouette it cast against the sky was quite aesthetic).

So far, the war had been mostly guerrilla; mostly attacks on supplies and infrastructure; nothing organised, nothing... violent. So if he pretended like he couldn't see the fey, perhaps they'd ignore him, pass on by. They were glamoured, after all, which meant they didn't *want* to be seen.

Dave's pulse pounded at his ears as his memory dredged up the contract he'd signed—in particular, the final clause. If he passed, if he was hired, the job came with excellent death benefits, to be paid out to his next of kin, or whomever he decided to nominate.

Suppose I have to survive first.

The fey halted a mere three paces away, staring at him. Dave fought back the shiver that tried to rattle through him, adrenalin skipping his heart along like a hummingbird on the periphery of a storm.

"Shall I kill him?" the darker male said, voice low and angry.

Something in Dave rose at that; if he'd hackles, perhaps they'd have risen too.

What right did the fey have to be angry? *They* weren't the ones who'd had their homes invaded, who'd been harried and terrorised by beings stronger and more powerful than them, who had sat alone in a room and baked in their own sweat, empty stomach curling in on itself for days on end in the heat of a brown-out.

Bile rose in Dave's throat.

Easy. Steady now. Don't let them know you know.

The female shifted, holding a hand up in the universally recognised 'stop' gesture. "He senses something," she hissed.

"Then let me deal with him," the male said.

A flickering caught the edge of Dave's eye.

He fought not to look.

Something… green.

Sparkling. Glittering away on the male fey's arm.

Externally, nothing changed; internally, David swore as his mind leapt into top gear.

Green, shimmering, arm of the fey...

He swore again. A dragon.

It had to be a dragon, right there on the arm of the fey, writhing and shimmering and twisting, catching the last faint glow of twilight. Or was it giving off its own light, and that's why it looked brighter now that it was nearly dark?

Dave swallowed—he couldn't help it, and they would either kill him or leave him alone in a second anyway, the female one had realised he could sense them, no point pretending now.

But... A dragon...

The only thing going for him was the element of surprise.

He leapt at the male fey with the iridescent green dragon twining around his arm like a living tattoo.

The female one splayed her hand.

Pain smacked Dave across the face; he spat blood.

One finger. He'd heard that was all it took. Just one touch of his skin against the dragon, and he could convince it to come to him—and he could *live*.

The male fey pivoted back, bared his teeth, raised the wrist that bore the dragon—

And the female slammed her arm in front of him, pinning him back. "Akash," she said, immovable. "No."

Dave wasn't going to waste time worrying about what she meant. He leapt, feinting a high dive—and switching at the last second to a low grab.

He dove below the female's outstretched arm and swept the male's legs out from under him.

They smacked into the dirt. Clouds of it puffed up in the almost-dark, living shadows that clogged Dave's mouth, nose.

He coughed the taste of it away. Clawed his way up the fey's leg, fingers wrapping in the loose, billowing fabric of his pants.

The fey kicked out—one foot caught Dave's nose.

Hot pain blinded him. He hissed as the metallic tang of blood filled his mouth.

Didn't let go. Didn't stop moving.

His only chance of getting out of this alive was the dragon.

The female screamed something, and Dave's back seized, cramping tight and bowing his spine.

He didn't let go.

The fey kicked, jackrabbiting on the ground.

Dave got his feet under him.

Leapt.

Landed on the fey male's torso in a short dive. The momentum carried

Dave over the other side, and now the male fey was blocking him from the female, and his vision flared with green.

Blood! Blood blood blood blood blood.

A voice of smoke and ash in his mind.

Yes! Dave screamed back at the voice in his head. *Blood!*

It was all he could taste, all he could smell, his face sticky and wet with it in the new night air.

And if he'd thought he'd known pain before, it was nothing compared to the agony that exploded up his arm now.

His body went rigid, hands flexing. *Blood blood blood.*

Something hot, sharp—indescribable agony—twisting and twining and writhing—up his arm, to his neck, his face.

The sensation of something licking at his nose—*from the inside.*

Dave shuddered. Bit back a scream.

His face was glowing dragon-green.

The fey female was shouting, screaming, the male pounding his fists at Dave's legs, his ribs—

But that pain was dim, distant, compared to the searing, exquisite agony of the dragon feeding from the fresh blood on his face.

Blood blood blood.

Yes, Dave replied, and even in his head his voice seemed ragged, gasping. *You can have more if you stop them hurting me.*

A mental image of a dragon grin, all long, white fangs and glittering eyes.

Something wound tight around his neck.

Dave gasped. Scrabbled at it. Nothing there, nothing but skin.

The air seemed to tighten as well, air pressure increasing until his ears felt like they were going to pop, like being crushed under the weight of a thousand buildings, like suffocating with air still in your lungs.

The pressure, the pain…

…exploded.

Outward.

Away from him.

And when his vision cleared and the pain receded, all he could see in the full dark of night was the dull green shimmer through his grey shirt of the dragon, curled up under Dave's own skin, resting right over his heart—and the incapacitated bodies of two fey, sprawled awkwardly on the ground beneath the black-barked eucalypt like children's discarded play things.

Dave gasped at the air, still hot, even without the sun.

Touched his fingers lightly to his broken nose—they came away sticky with blood, but there was less than there should have been.

The dragon had literally taken it somehow.

Dave shuddered at that.

Gasped again as pain arrowed through him.

Straightened slowly, heart kicking fit to burst.

The fey never moved.

Fully upright, Dave snorted out his nose to clear the blood. Spat a metallic mouthful of the stuff onto the dirt beneath the stars. Realised just how fierce a beating the fey male had given him—maybe a cracked rib or two. He was going to limp for days.

But.

He grinned fiercely in response. Touched his shirt front.

He had a dragon.

If that wasn't worth a steady pay cheque, he didn't know what was.

And so, a little unsteady on his feet and with one hand cradling the dragon that slept under the skin of his left pec, Dave spat at the fey again for good measure, turned, and headed back to town.

He'd lived. He'd seen the fey, and he'd lived.

The pay might even cover the medical bill.

THE MAKING OF
RECRUITMENT

Oooh, *Recruitment*. I do have a soft spot for this story, partly because David and Akash are named for real people whom I adore, but also partly because something about the setting of this story really appeals to me. In my mind, it's so vivid it's like somewhere I've visited in real life.

I love everything about this world: the heat, the dust, the tension between human and fey—and of course, the *beautiful* iridescent dragons that wind in and out of this world like tattoos on skin, something integral to but also separate from, something intimately a part of the person they are tattooed on, but also a thing apart, ink instead of dermal cells, azo instead of melanin—

and in this world, alien instead of either human *or* fey.

All of which is to say, I love this world, known currently as *The Fey Wars* world, and have Grand Plans for it. If you'd like to read more, you can grab a copy of *It All Changes Now*, which contains three *Fey Wars* stories, or you can head to Free Stories on my website, which has a link to two of the *Fey Wars* stories available on my blog for free. In the meantime, I hope you enjoyed *Recruitment*.

Read more by Amy Laurens!

THE MULTIVERSE MAY BURN

"That's enough." The judge, in her stylised white wig and long navy robes, didn't shout, but she didn't need to. Her gaze—not baby, not cornflower, not sky, but rather poison-dart frog, or cavernous ice, or man 'o war—over the top of her black-rimmed glasses was severe, the gaze of a woman who'd seen far too many trouble-makers in her life for even a molecule of sympathy to remain in her blood.

Alissa shivered. Before, she'd thought that maybe, if she'd come in with a good enough story and a water-tight argument, she might have had a chance. But that look from the judge brokered no compromise, and Alissa looked quickly away, studying the flecks of black in the white-marble floor tiles.

Tiny specks of silver shone, and for a moment Alissa thought that maybe they represented hope amid the black-and-white of the justice system. But that, surely, was too much to assume; the room stank of bleach so strongly they might as well have advertised, 'One courtroom, clean of germs and mercy both.'

Stomach twisting, Alissa raised her gaze to stare at the walls instead, more uncompromising white, except where the recording screens—panels as tall as she was, as wide as her arm-span—interrupted them.

Three of the viewing screens were currently in use. From one, a severe-faced man with salt-and-pepper hair and deep, deep lines in his dark skin frowned down at her. In another, the cyborg Natia Alchamp narrowed their hazel eyes, lightly-tanned fist clench-ing in front of them on the dark-wood desk they sat behind, occasional flares of colour coalescent around their head as they used their implant to access the multiverse.

And in the third…

Alissa swallowed heavily.

In the third, the most beautiful man she'd ever seen sat scowling at her, dark eyes full of something she could only assume was hatred. Two long, red scratches puckered his brown cheek and at the sight of them again, Alissa's stomach clenched, adrenalin punching through her system.

She could taste that blood in her mouth, metallic, sweet, and if anyone here thought she would ever be sorry for what she'd done, they had another thing coming.

She'd die first.

Literally, and they would be the ones to kill her.

Which, damn it all, it wasn't her *fault. They* were the ones who'd fed her mother Rapunzel in the first place, hoping for yet another super-powered child to join their ranks.

So how was it Alissa's fault if things had gone slightly wrong—assuming a spontaneous genetic mutation could be considered 'wrong'?

"It is obvious that you are as stubborn as you are articulate," the judge continued, as a school teacher disciplining an unruly child might. "But your arguments are irrelevant. The fact of the matter is that you not only possess the forbidden blood magic, you actively chose to use it on this man."

Alissa's nostrils flared. Curse Hannah. Curse the witches. Curse everyone involved with her birth—and most of all, herself. Alissa drew in a steely breath, the unforgiving bleach filling her awareness.

Well, so would she be. Unforgiving, resolved, and devoid of mercy. If they were going to sentence her to death for possessing a talent she hadn't asked for, didn't want, then by the Clans she'd go down swinging and take them all with her.

She snorted. Folded her arms. Raised her chin and stared back at the fair-skinned woman who thought herself worthy to lay judgement on this matter.

The judge narrowed her own eyes in return. "Well then, Alissa Fortuna McAlister. You have brought this fate upon yourself. You have admitted to wielding blood magic in an act of aggression against another human being, as if possessing the red magic wasn't bad enough—and we have seen recorded evidence that your magic glows red instead of blue, as it ought. You know the penalty for this is death."

Adrenalin pulsed again, this time with a sour squirt of acid in the back of her throat. Alissa coughed, trying to swallow away the burn.

This was it, then. This was the end,

and she'd take them all with her—

She felt both magics, the sanctioned blue and the unsanctioned red, rising in her body, one cold and sharp like a migraine, one hot and tingling like pins and needles, a metallic taste rising in the back of her throat like blood, if blood were copper-blue instead of iron-red.

She couldn't do anything about Raiden, who'd dobbed her in and thus effectively signed her death warrant himself, and that... well, that pissed her off, to be honest.

But the judge was going to be sorry.

"*Unless.*" The judge pursed her blue-painted lips, so bright they made her skin seem pale as death, so bright they outshone her gleaming eyes. "Someone will speak for you, and agree to complete a Multiverse Trial."

Keep reading! Head to
www.inkprintpress.com/
amylaurens/
itallchangesnow/
to buy your copy now!

ABOUT THE AUTHOR

AMY LAURENS is an Australian author of fantasy fiction for all ages. Her story *Bones Of The Sea*, about creepy carnivorous mist and bone curses, won the 2021 Aurealis Award for Best Fantasy Novella.

Amy has also written the award-winning portal-fantasy *Sanctuary* series about Edge, a 13-year-old girl forced to move to a small country town because of witness protection (the first book is *Where Shadows Rise*), the humorous fantasy *Kaditeos* series, following newly graduated Evil Overlord Mercury as she attempts to acquire a castle, the young adult series *Storm Foxes*, about love and magic and family in small town Australia, and a whole host of non-fiction.

INKLETS

Collect them all! Released on the 1st and 15th of each month.

Dancer, Dreamer
Seer
LIANA BROOKS

As Time
Whirls Slowly
Past
AMY LAURENS

Far More
Satisfying
Than Hell
AMY LAURENS

Just
Another Day
In Hell
LIANA BROOKS

Moon AND
Morning
AMY LAURENS

Some
Impropriety
Expected
AMY LAURENS

NEON SNOW
LIANA BROOKS

Reincarnation
LIANA BROOKS

More Than
Mushrooms
AMY LAURENS

DOUBLE ISSUE
INKLET #002
How To Make A Star
& The World Ended
LIANA BROOKS

INKLET #003
CAUGHT
IN THE ACT
AMY LAURENS

INKLET #004
ANUBIS
Has Sent You
Six Souls
LIANA BROOKS

INKLET #005
PRAYER TO A
GODDESS
LIANA BROOKS

INKLET #006
Love In The
Time Of Corona
AMY LAURENS

INKLET #007
RECRUITMENT
AMY LAURENS

INKLET #008
IDENTITY
Theft 101
LIANA BROOKS

INKLET #009
Curses
With Benefits
AMY LAURENS

INKLET #100
NECROMANCER
TROUBLES
LIANA BROOKS